YOU ARE OK!
OCD Is Not Who You Are

The content associated with this book is the sole work and responsibility of the author. Gatekeeper Press had no involvement in the generation of this content.

You Are OK!
OCD Is Not Who You Are

Published by Gatekeeper Press
7853 Gunn Hwy., Suite 209
Tampa, FL 33626
www.GatekeeperPress.com

Copyright © 2024 by Frankie D,

All rights reserved. Neither this book, nor any parts within it may be sold or reproduced in any form or by any electronic or mechanical means, including information storage and retrieval systems, without permission in writing from the author. The only exception is by a reviewer, who may quote short excerpts in a review.

The cover design, typesetting, and editorial work for this book are entirely the product of the author. Gatekeeper Press did not participate in and is not responsible for any aspect of these elements.

ISBN (paperback): 9781662952722

YOU ARE OK!
OCD Is Not Who You Are

Frankie D.

Illustrated by ....

gatekeeper press
Tampa, Florida

DEDICATION

To K. R. D-B my inspiration, my dream come true.
I will love you always & forever. Mama.

This is me at around 5 years old when my OCD started.

YOU ARE OK!

INTRODUCTION

I wrote this book for you to know you are OK and not alone. So, let's take this journey and create this book together.
I left the pages blank for your drawings of whatever comes to mind after you read my words.
Don't forget to add your name next to "Illustrated by".
You never know what amazing things you can create until you try!

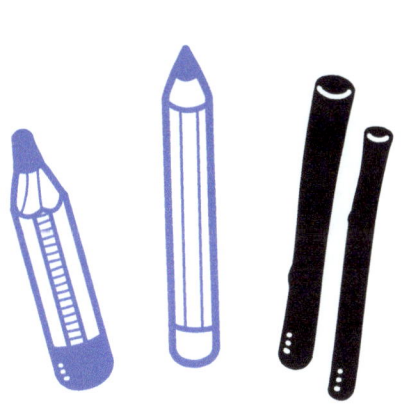 

I want you to know you are okay.
Your brain just works in a different way.

This is your space to create

These thoughts are not you.
It is just something your brain does because
it thinks it needs to protect you
when it really doesn't need to.

This is your space to create

I know it can be scary.
But your thoughts are just your thoughts.
They are not who you are.

This is your space to create

Who you are is what's inside and how you act.
Like how you play, love your family and friends,
and how you treat your pets.
That is who you are.

This is your space to create

So don't ever be afraid to tell your family what's going on.
They can help you move along.
Remember, the thoughts are not here to stay,
and sharing them can help them go away.

This is your space to create

I want you to know you are okay.
Your brain just works in a different way.

This is your space to create

YOU ARE LOVED!

If you would like to share your drawings with me,
with your parents permission and their help,
email them to HelpLove07@gmail.com
They will not ever be shared without direct permission.

A huge thank you to Alexandra Andries for her care
and compassion in helping to create this book of comfort
and love for those with OCD. You are appreciated!

www.ingramcontent.com/pod-product-compliance
Lightning Source LLC
LaVergne TN
LVHW070119080526
838200LV00080B/4702